Aron Runs for Class President

Written by Nahjee Grant

Illustrated by Justine Babcock

This book is dedicated to the memory of Sierra Bailey

When Aron returns from his trip to the White House to meet President Obama, he joyfully shares pictures of his adventure with his classmates.

His friends are eager to hear stories from a once-in-a-lifetime opportunity to time-travel with the president.

Before class is over, Aron's history teacher, Ms. Pry, announces elections for class president will take place in two weeks and any student who's interested to step forward by the end of class.

With a growing smile on his face, Aron sits at his desk glancing at a portrait of Obama and pondering the opportunity to run for office like his idol.

"I would like to run!" Aron says enthusiastically as he approaches his teacher's desk.

Another student walks to the desk and says he will run also. Barry is a popular athlete and captain of the soccer team, Aron looks unflattered by his decision to run.

Ms. Pry explains the rules for the election and advises them to be mindful to respect each other's campaign. Aron pays close attention, but Barry doesn't seem to take it as seriously.

Aron slips his backpack on and rushes towards the door, excited to get started on his campaign.

He returns home after school to tell his parents the great news about the campaign and how he will make history like Barack Obama by becoming the first African American class president in school history.

Aron's father explains to him that with hard work, dedication, good grades, and a commitment to help others, he can achieve anything he sets his heart on.

Eager to play outside, Aron looks out the window and sees his friends playing at the park.

Understanding his responsibilities come first, Aron heads back to the computer to work on his campaign plan. He understands his friends will always be there once his goal is achieved and makes sure that his homework is complete first before researching successful campaign strategies.

Aron researches how much money is needed to buy campaign materials such as signs and posters, so he organizes a lemonade stand outside the cafeteria to raise money.

In just two days, the fundraiser is a huge success and enough money is raised to buy yard signs which Aron places outside the school entrance.

Every day when it is time for recess, Aron skips playing with his friends and speaks to classmates one on one about the issues they care most about and takes notes.

After school, he attends faculty and staff meetings to voice his opinion and address his classmates' concerns from the information he collects.

Throughout the day, on his way to class, Aron passes out campaign flyers to classmates in the hallway which detail his campaign promises and a short biography about himself.

Ms. Pry approaches Aron to tell him to keep his head up and move forward with his campaign no matter what people may think of him. Aron feels a bit upset but still optimistic.

Aron regains his confidence and organizes a rally in the cafeteria to share his plans for the school year. Standing on a lunch table, he enthusiastically addresses the crowd as to why he is the best candidate to get the job done as president.

On the last day of campaigning, Aron is posting a flyer in the hallway when Barry approaches him. He arrogantly indicates that he doesn't have to work hard to win, because he's more popular and knows more students than Aron.

Finally home from the last day of campaigning, Aron walks in the door extremely tired. In just two short weeks he has managed to meet and greet every student, organize a fundraiser to raise money to post signs and flyers all over the school, and sacrifice playing with his friends while still staying focused on his school work.

Before Aron completes his homework and gets ready for bed, his parents let him know he gave it his best effort and they are so very proud of him no matter what the results of the election.

Aron remembers the encouraging words President Obama said during his White House visit to follow his heart, he strongly believes the president is proud of him.

It is finally Election Day and Aron greets every classmate at the door before they make their final decision.

Students began to stand in line to vote for their new president by writing the candidate's name on a piece of paper and dropping it in the ballot box.

Aron nervously chews his pencil waiting for the results to be announced and hoping all of his hard work has paid off.

Much to his surprise, Barry approaches Aron to tell him he ran a great campaign and that he respects Aron's hard work. Aron shakes his hand and thanks Barry for stepping up to serve and represent the class.

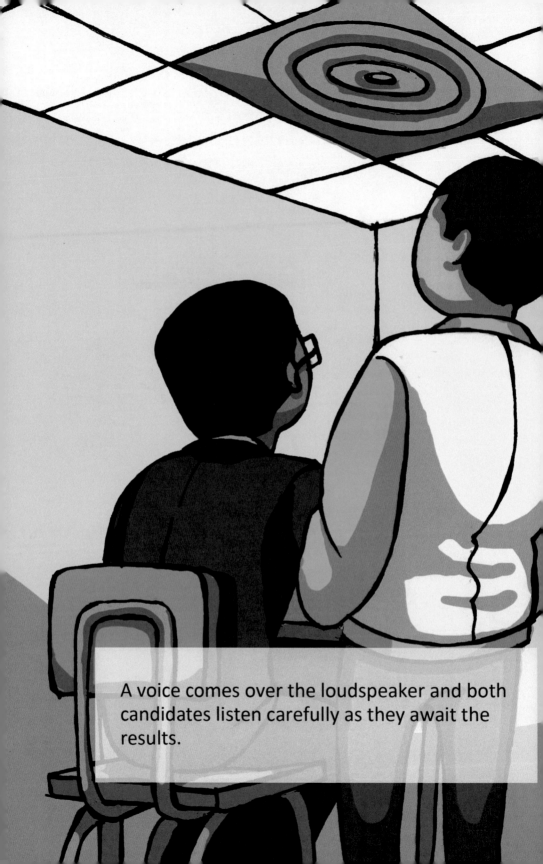

A voice comes over the loudspeaker and both candidates listen carefully as they await the results.

The speaker announces Aron has won the election. His supporters cheerfully chant his name ARON! ARON! He is still stunned as he is now class president.

Ms. Pry calls Aron to the front of the classroom and presents him with a ceremonial gavel to preside over class meetings and announces he is the first African American class president in school history.

At lunchtime, President Aron delivers his acceptance speech and expresses how hard he will work to serve as class president for every student, whether they voted for him or not.

The crowd begins to cheer with excitement for so long, many of them missed their lunch period.

Aron gets home from school and energetically runs into the house with a big smile on his face.

Happy to share the great news with his parents, they congratulate him on his victory and remind him that he can achieve anything he sets his mind to.